hen

Who is in the field?

a TUFFY book™
FARM BABIES

read it • chew it • wash it • love it

Hello! Hello! Let's meet the new babies on the farm!

chicks

horse

foal

Who is in the barn?

cat

kittens

owl

owlets

Who is at the pond?

duck

ducklings

turtle

hatchlings

Who is in the garden?

kits

rabbit